I0830767

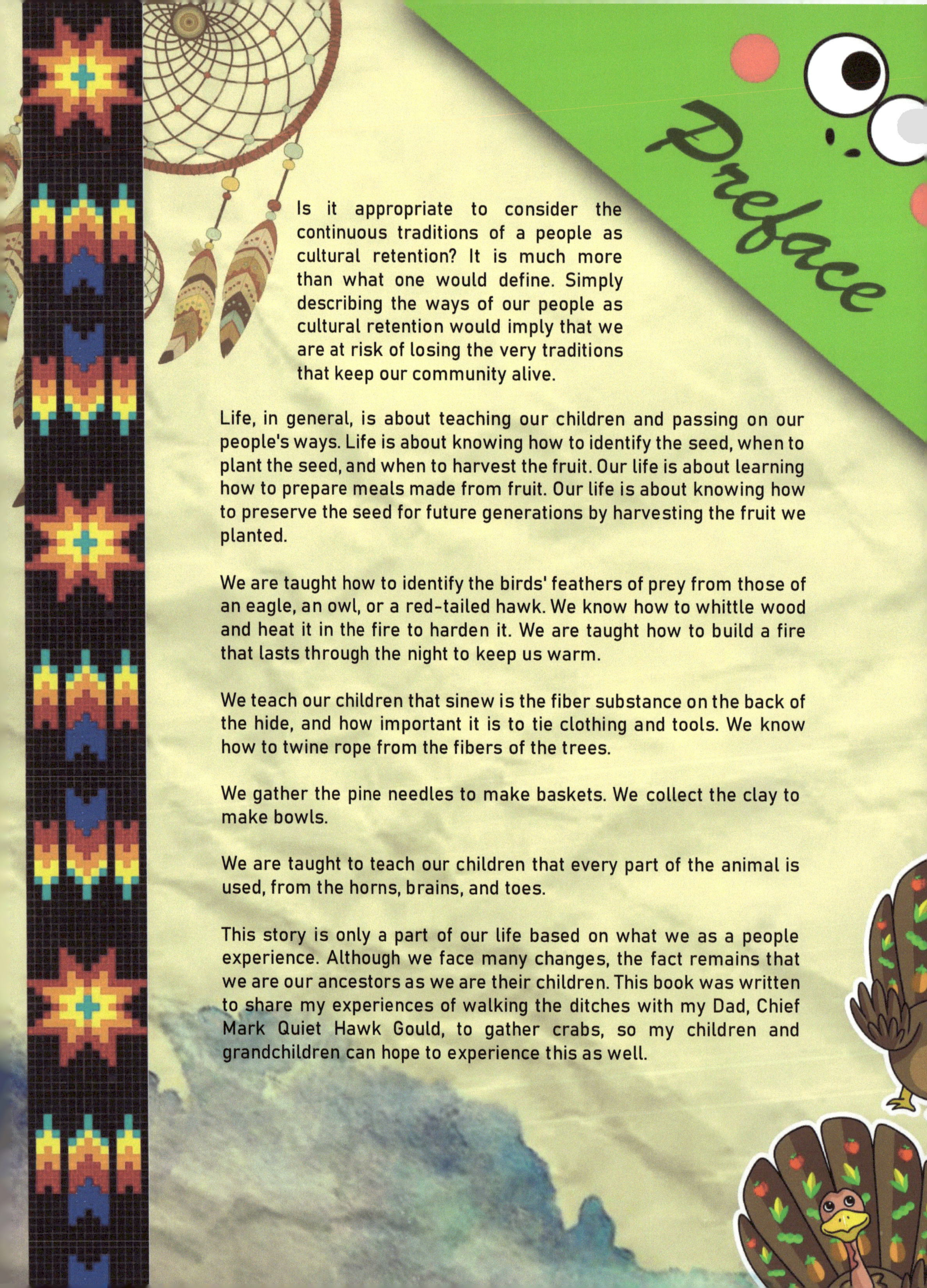

Is it appropriate to consider the continuous traditions of a people as cultural retention? It is much more than what one would define. Simply describing the ways of our people as cultural retention would imply that we are at risk of losing the very traditions that keep our community alive.

Life, in general, is about teaching our children and passing on our people's ways. Life is about knowing how to identify the seed, when to plant the seed, and when to harvest the fruit. Our life is about learning how to prepare meals made from fruit. Our life is about knowing how to preserve the seed for future generations by harvesting the fruit we planted.

We are taught how to identify the birds' feathers of prey from those of an eagle, an owl, or a red-tailed hawk. We know how to whittle wood and heat it in the fire to harden it. We are taught how to build a fire that lasts through the night to keep us warm.

We teach our children that sinew is the fiber substance on the back of the hide, and how important it is to tie clothing and tools. We know how to twine rope from the fibers of the trees.

We gather the pine needles to make baskets. We collect the clay to make bowls.

We are taught to teach our children that every part of the animal is used, from the horns, brains, and toes.

This story is only a part of our life based on what we as a people experience. Although we face many changes, the fact remains that we are our ancestors as we are their children. This book was written to share my experiences of walking the ditches with my Dad, Chief Mark Quiet Hawk Gould, to gather crabs, so my children and grandchildren can hope to experience this as well.

THIS BOOK belongs to

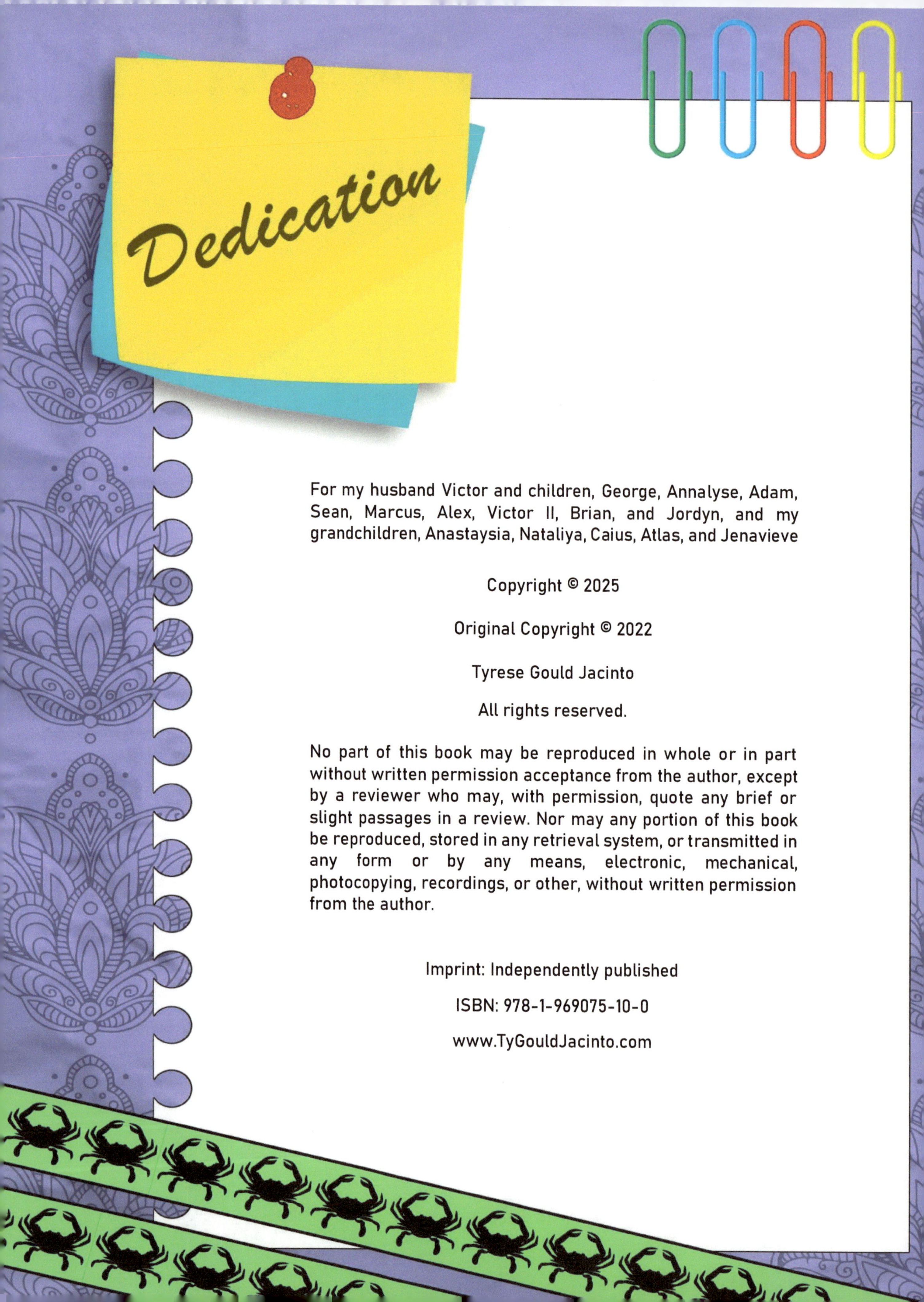

For my husband Victor and children, George, Annalyse, Adam, Sean, Marcus, Alex, Victor II, Brian, and Jordyn, and my grandchildren, Anastaysia, Nataliya, Caius, Atlas, and Jenavieve

Imprint: Independently published

ISBN: 978-1-969075-10-0

www.TyGouldJacinto.com

Precious
Cohanzick
Lenape
Crabs
Tyrese Gould Jacinto
Art by Arnild C. Aldepolla

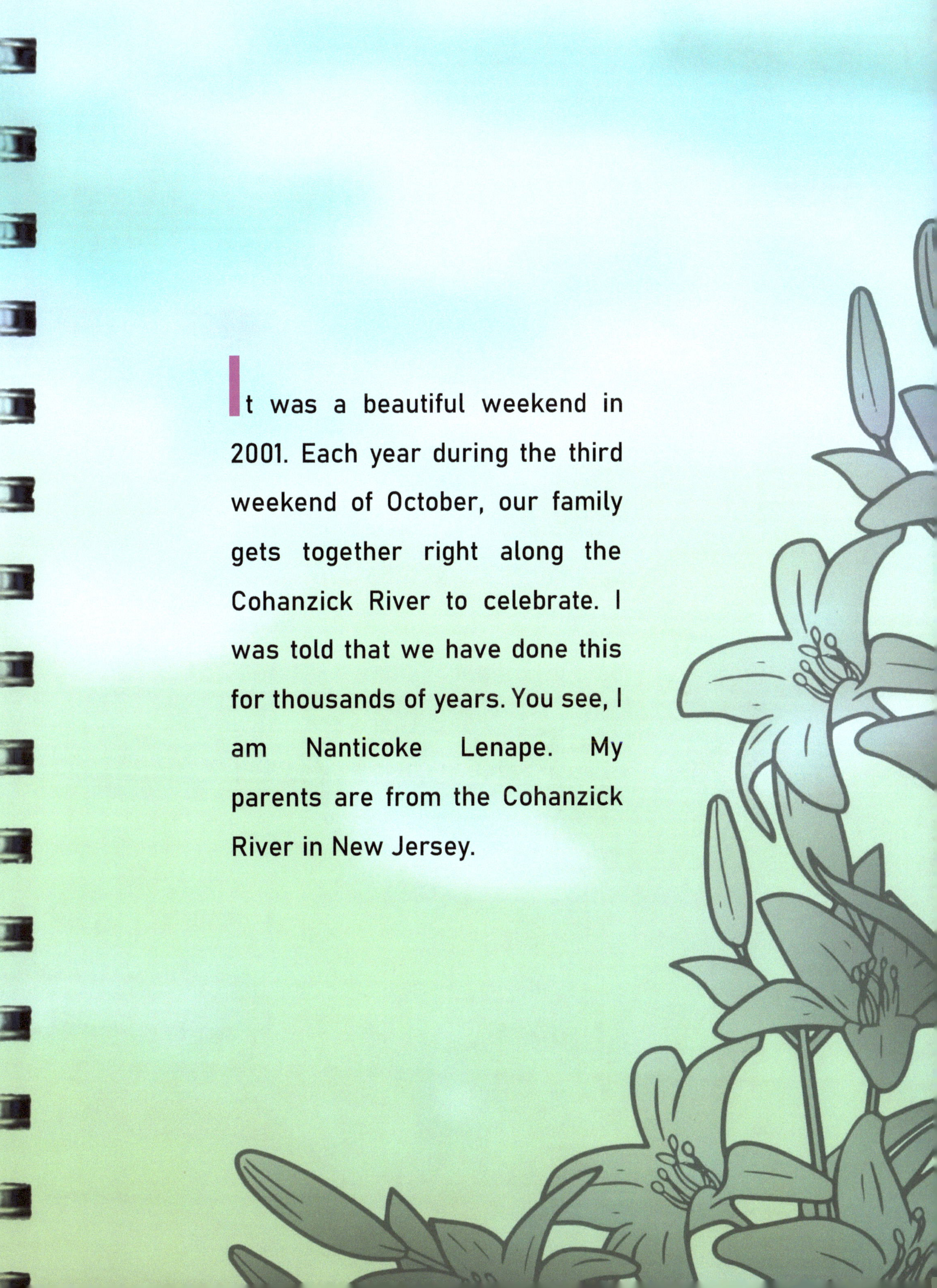

It was a beautiful weekend in 2001. Each year during the third weekend of October, our family gets together right along the Cohanzick River to celebrate. I was told that we have done this for thousands of years. You see, I am Nanticoke Lenape. My parents are from the Cohanzick River in New Jersey.

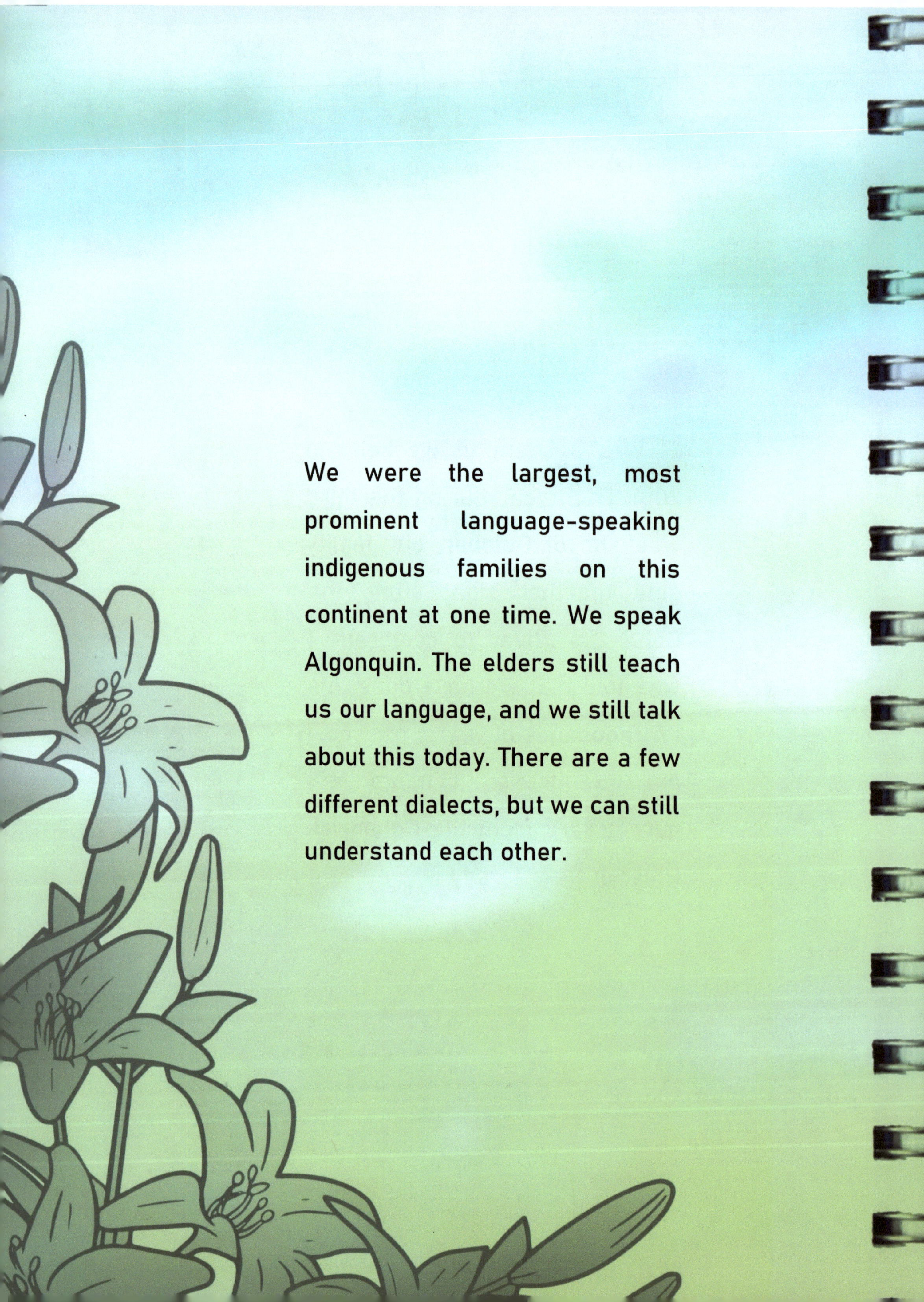

We were the largest, most prominent language-speaking indigenous families on this continent at one time. We speak Algonquin. The elders still teach us our language, and we still talk about this today. There are a few different dialects, but we can still understand each other.

scrapbook

We are matriarchal, which means we live with our mother's people. So, when you are married, you leave your family and live with your wife's family if you are a man.

We call the elderly females of our family Toma; this name means that she is the keeper of our wisdom and stories. She is a wise person who helps with family matters and healing. We always revere females in our family with high regard and respect.

My name is Tanah "Lily Flower,"
and I am 30 years old. I
remember the family gathering in
2001 when I was in fourth grade,
which changed my life.

The weekend was beautiful. My emotions were high with excitement. As a child, the gathering on the Cohanzick River was the year's highlight. I was able to play with hundreds of cousins from Virginia, Maryland, Delaware, and New Jersey. Our family is big; there are many generations. As a matter of fact, there are nearly 7 generations this year.

I just loved spending time with my grandmother. She would tell me stories that her mother told her. Her stories were so enjoyable, and I would see myself in her story as she said them. I could smell the food and see the house as she described the past.

My grandmother knew so much about nature. She told me about the birds, plants, crabs, and perch fish that I loved to eat. She said that when she was little, there was plenty, and they were never hungry. They would gather the food when they needed to. They planted gardens and hunted as well.

Our families are considered "tide-water" families. For thousands of years, we lived in this area, the Cohanzick River, and gathered crabs, cleaned them by taking out the meat, dehydrated them in little drying huts, or carried them while they were alive to our homes. When we dehydrated the meat, we put it in leather bags to be used when we returned to our homes.

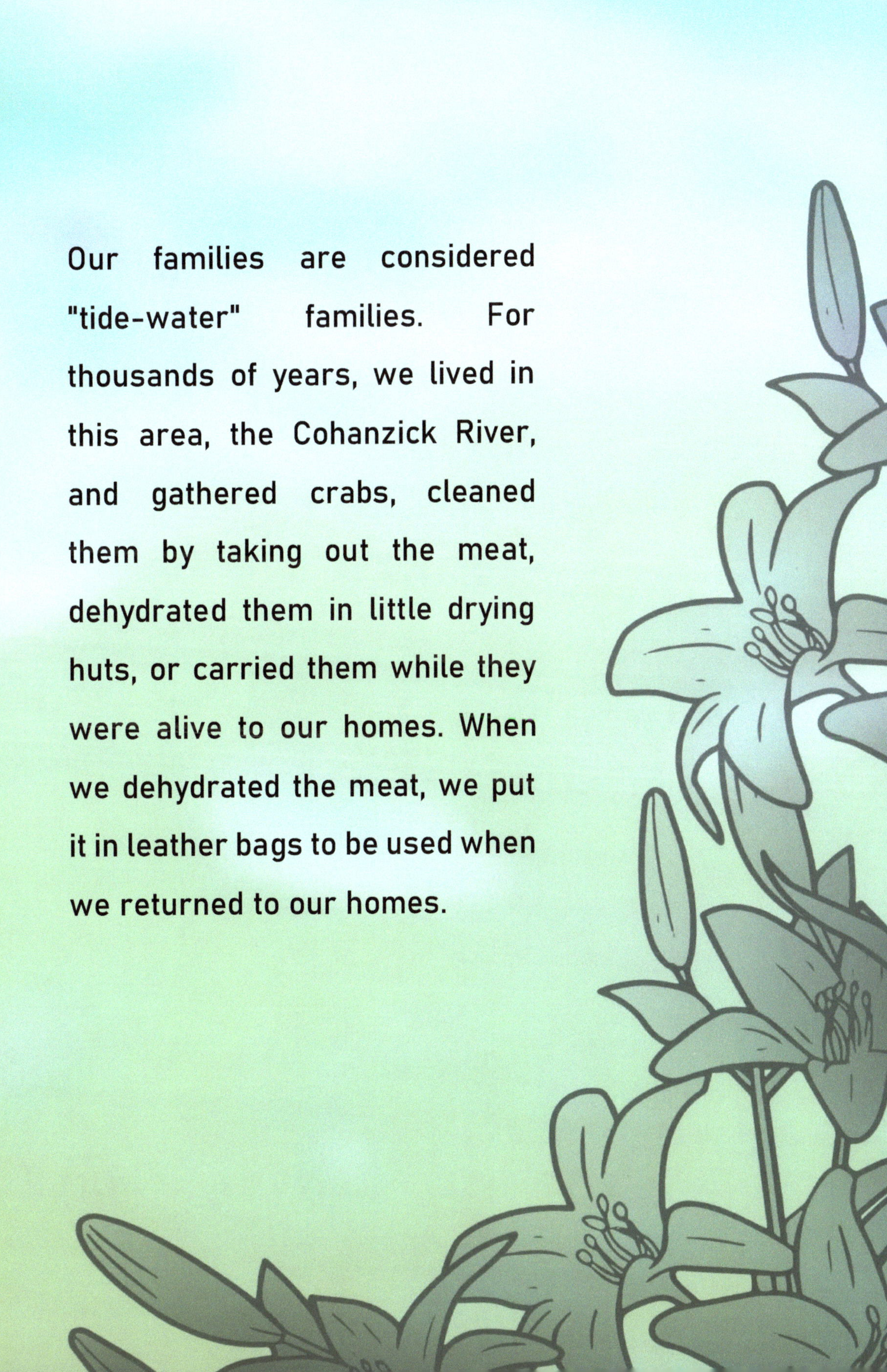

The year I was in fourth grade was special. I remember my great-grandmother sitting on a blanket near a closed area of the Cohanzick River. She sat looking directly at the roped area with the sign that stated, "Do not enter." Her hands were propped up on her bent knees and filled with the soil from where she was sitting.

DO NOT
ENTER!

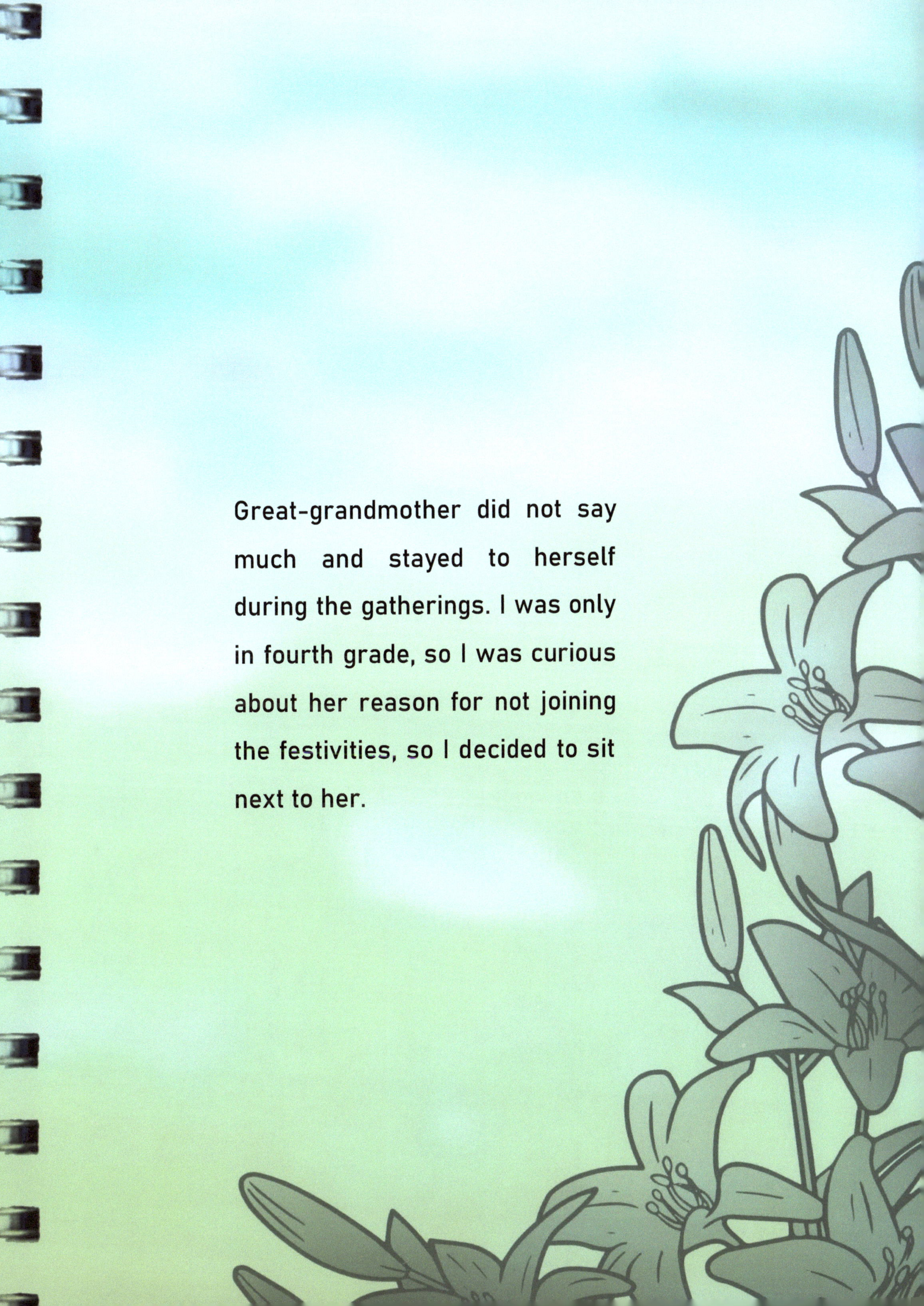

Great-grandmother did not say much and stayed to herself during the gatherings. I was only in fourth grade, so I was curious about her reason for not joining the festivities, so I decided to sit next to her.

When I looked at her, I noticed that she was not staring at the sign; however, her eyes were closed as if she were sleeping. She felt my presence, and a warm smile appeared on her face as she looked at me.

I was nervous, but I had to ask. "Uma, what are you doing?" I said. Uma means grandmother in Algonquin. Uma grabbed my hands, filled them with the warm soil, and told me the story that changed my life.

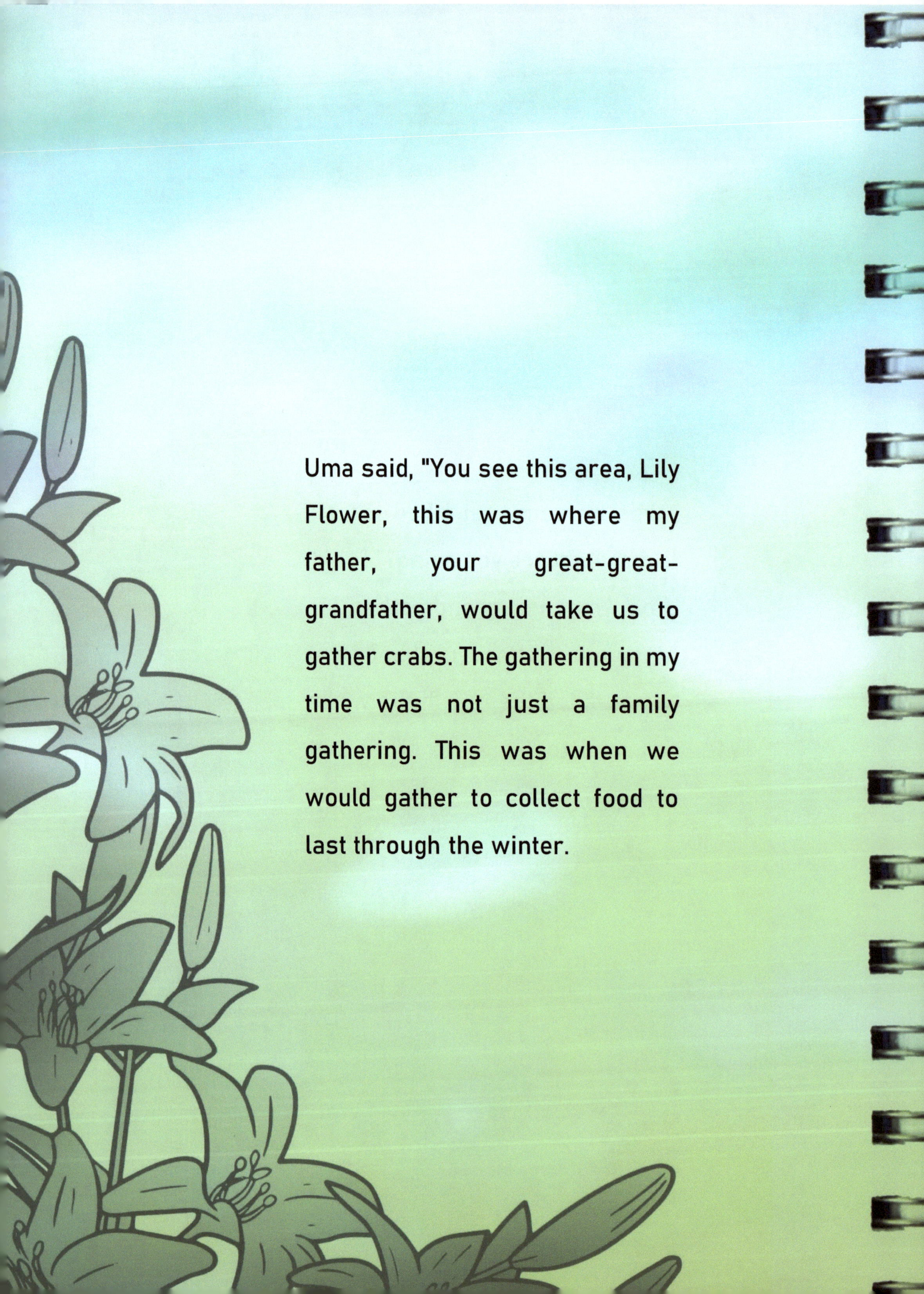

Uma said, "You see this area, Lily Flower, this was where my father, your great-great-grandfather, would take us to gather crabs. The gathering in my time was not just a family gathering. This was when we would gather to collect food to last through the winter.

We took the day-long journey, as did other families from around this area, and spent the week together, building dehydration huts, making baskets and nets, and walking the inlets where we would gather the crabs along the banks. The crabs were larger than those that we eat today. We were taught never to pick the crabs from the deep waters but only along the banks.

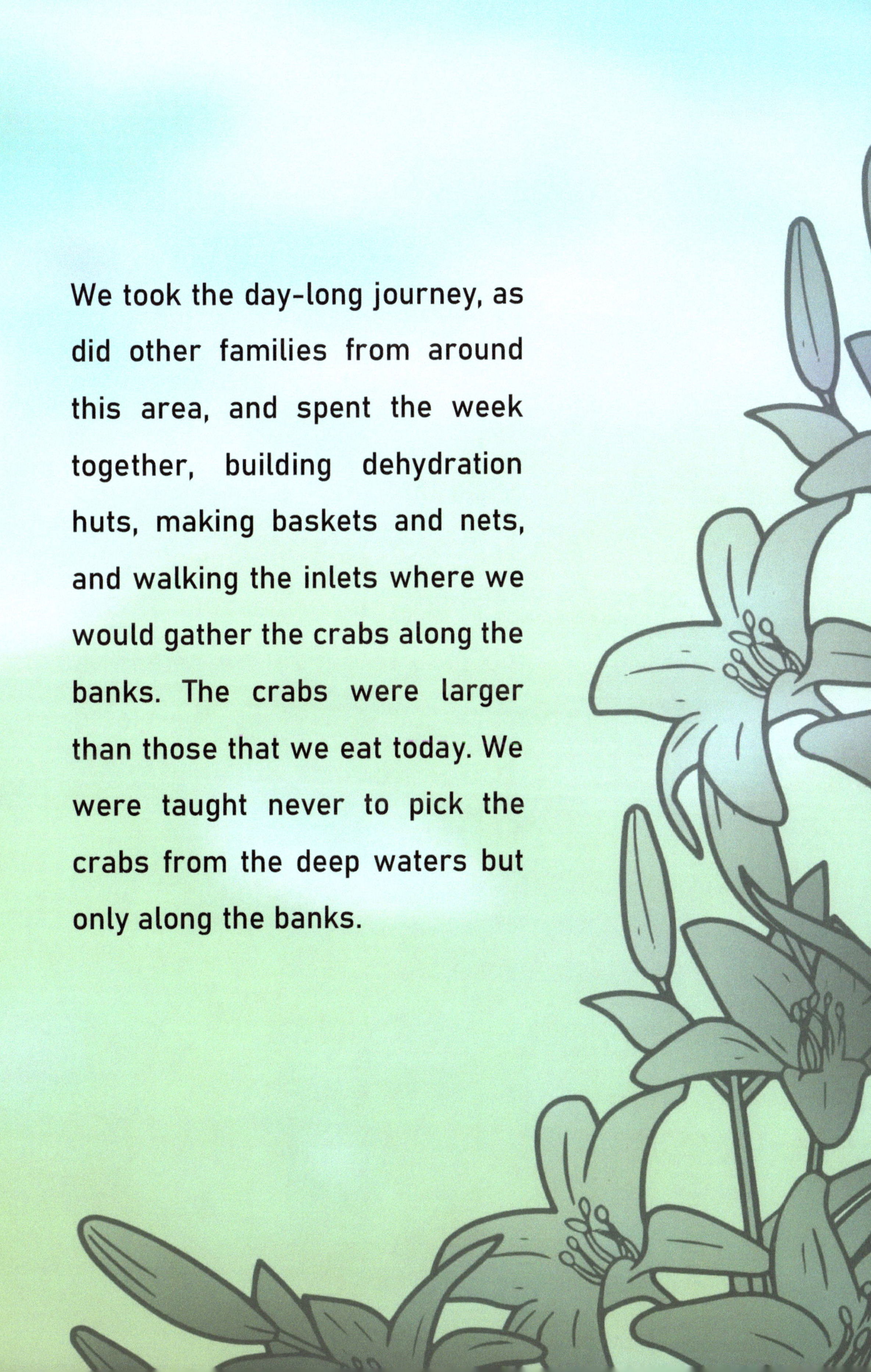

This area, which is now closed, is the main area where my father took our family to gather the crabs that we needed to last the winter. We walked for about half an hour with our baskets. This is the path to get to the gathering place during low tide. We would grab the crabs with our hands and nets when we arrived at the banks because the tide was low.

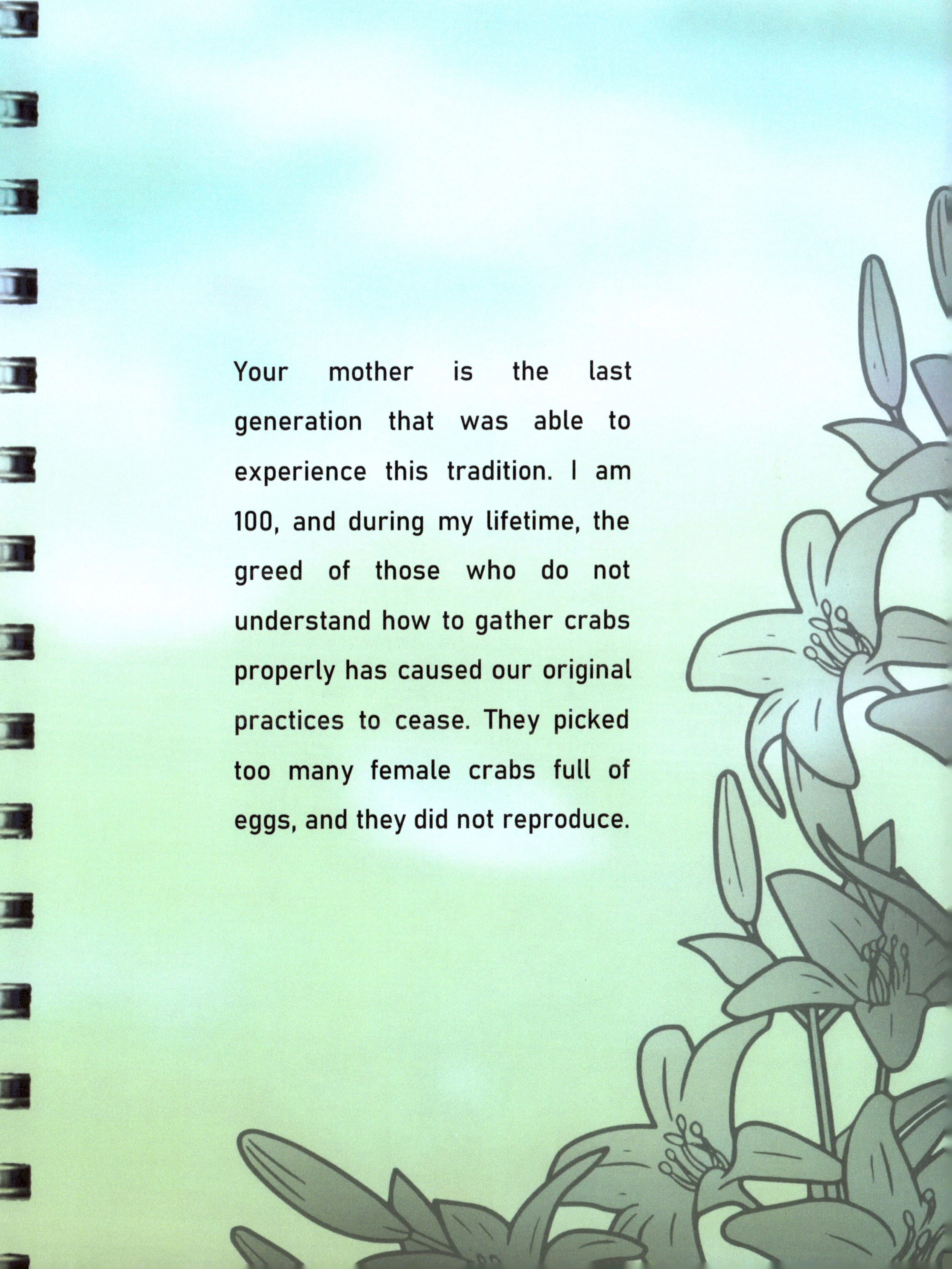

Your mother is the last generation that was able to experience this tradition. I am 100, and during my lifetime, the greed of those who do not understand how to gather crabs properly has caused our original practices to cease. They picked too many female crabs full of eggs, and they did not reproduce.

The new world has polluted our waters by dumping wastewater into the river. The fertilizer they use on the fields now runs into the river and bay with each rain, causing the fish and crabs to be smaller and even die.

When I hold this soil in my hand, I reflect on my experiences and meditate on how this can be better. I imagine this as a better place and wait patiently for the errors of man to be fixed.

This soil that you have in your hand is what holds your family's memories. I keep this soil and close my eyes, and I can see this memory and other stories told to me as a child. This soil has the water, the tears, and your family's footprint. You can see the stories I tell you when you hold this soil.

We can no longer gather the same way we had for thousands of years, and you are now the keeper of this story. You are the first to ask about this tradition, so you will now be responsible for keeping this story and more of our family."

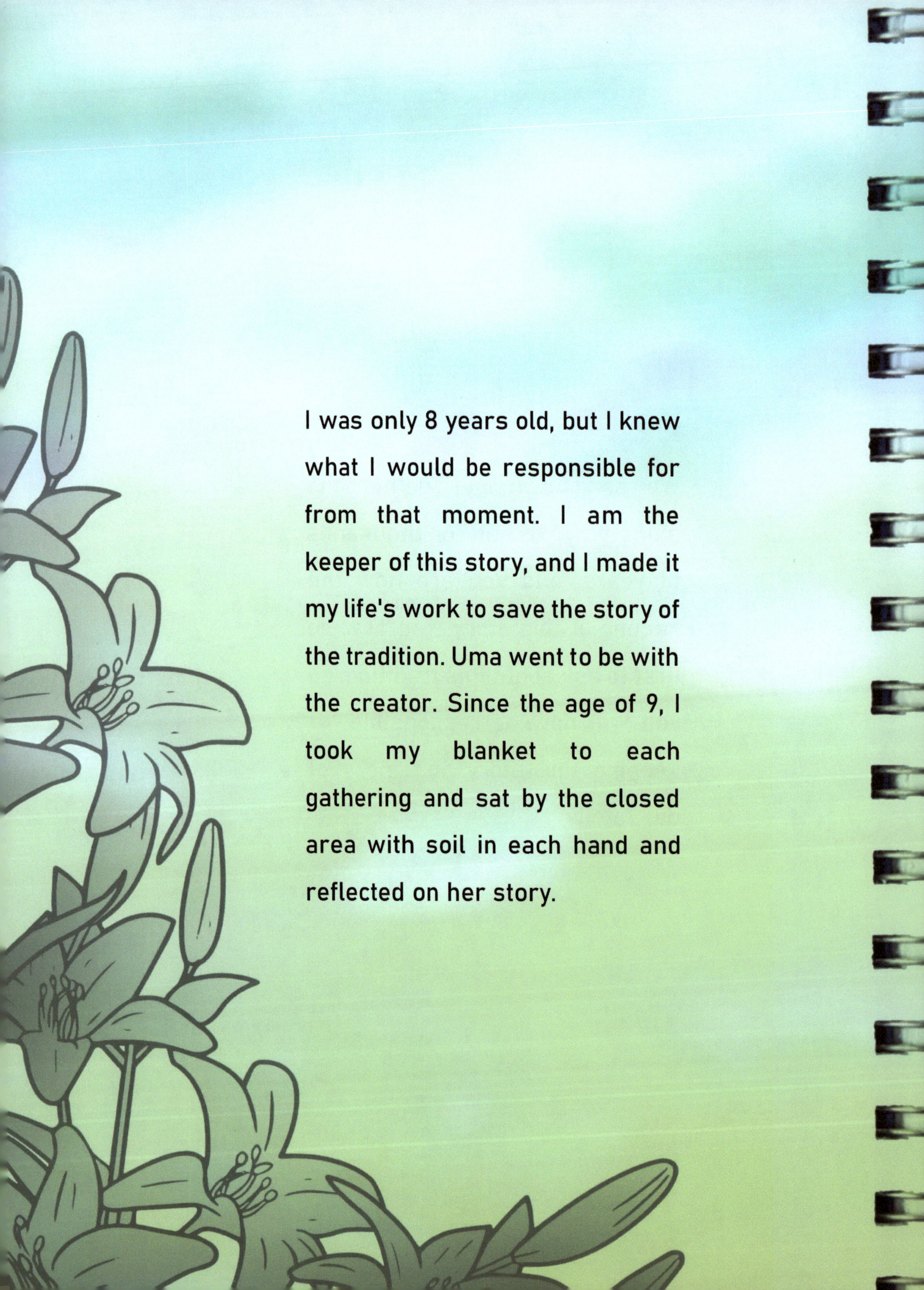

I was only 8 years old, but I knew what I would be responsible for from that moment. I am the keeper of this story, and I made it my life's work to save the story of the tradition. Uma went to be with the creator. Since the age of 9, I took my blanket to each gathering and sat by the closed area with soil in each hand and reflected on her story.

With Uma
Tanah
2022
TIDEWATER

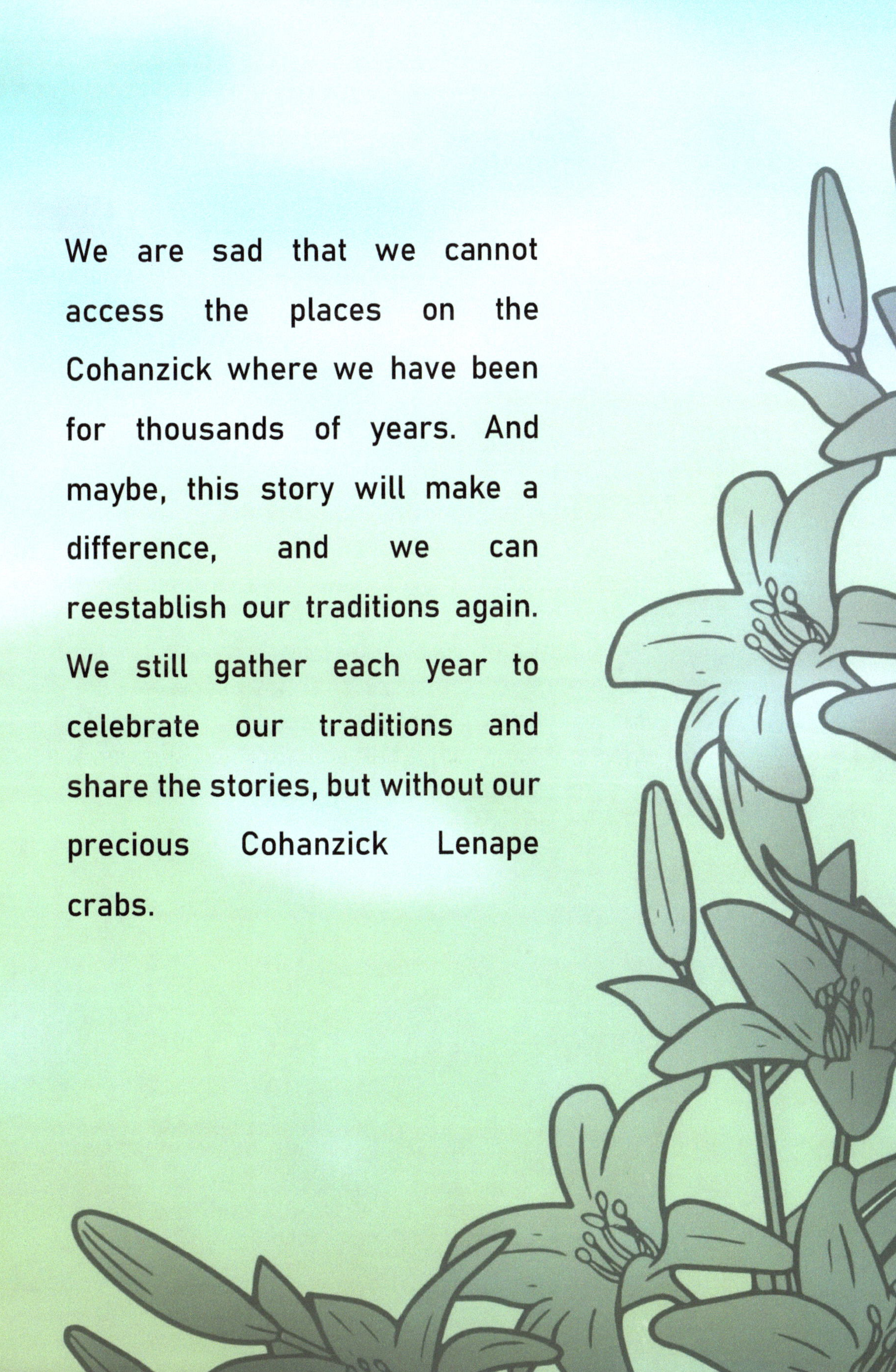

We are sad that we cannot access the places on the Cohanzick where we have been for thousands of years. And maybe, this story will make a difference, and we can reestablish our traditions again. We still gather each year to celebrate our traditions and share the stories, but without our precious Cohanzick Lenape crabs.

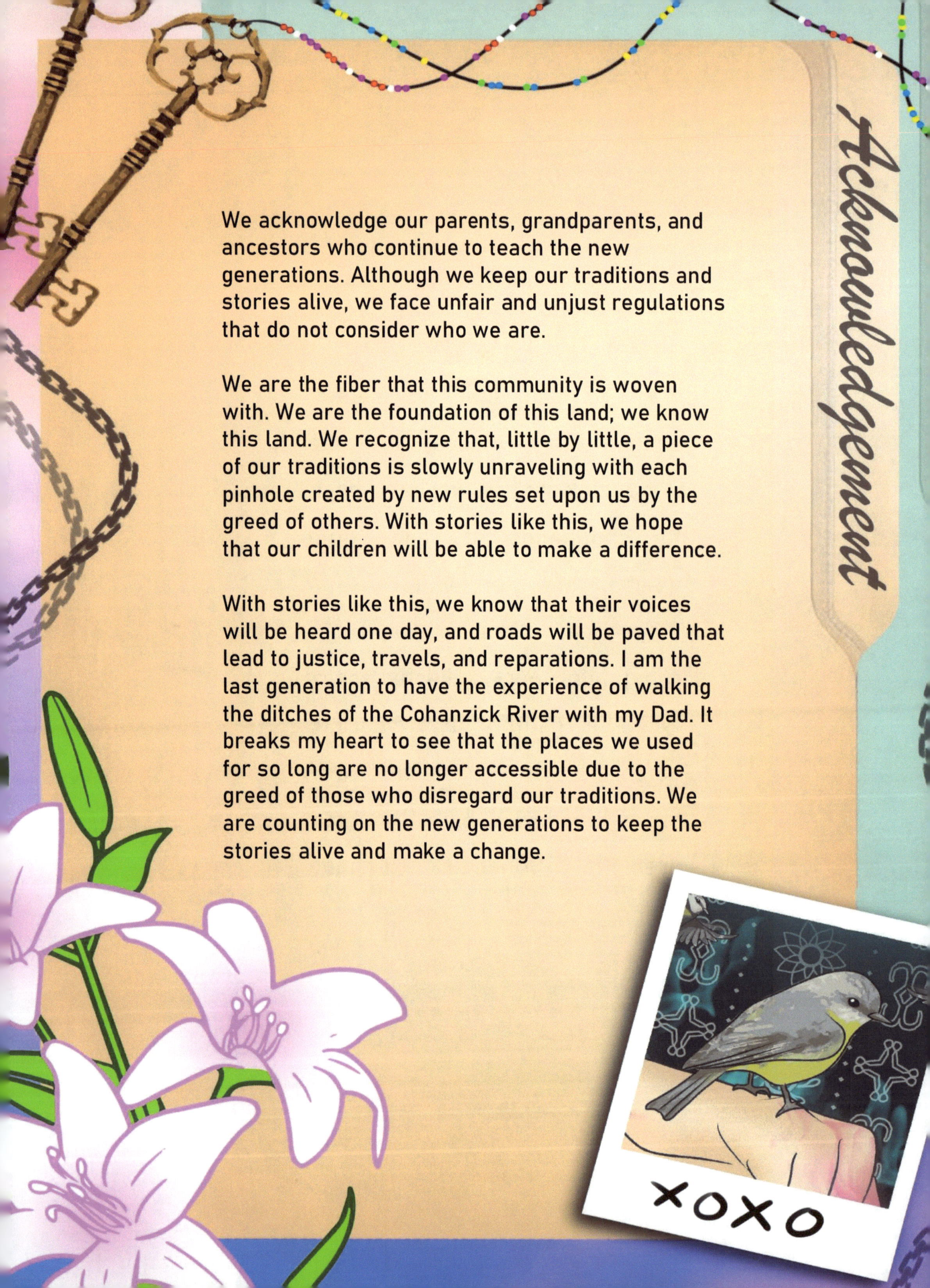

We acknowledge our parents, grandparents, and ancestors who continue to teach the new generations. Although we keep our traditions and stories alive, we face unfair and unjust regulations that do not consider who we are.

We are the fiber that this community is woven with. We are the foundation of this land; we know this land. We recognize that, little by little, a piece of our traditions is slowly unraveling with each pinhole created by new rules set upon us by the greed of others. With stories like this, we hope that our children will be able to make a difference.

With stories like this, we know that their voices will be heard one day, and roads will be paved that lead to justice, travels, and reparations. I am the last generation to have the experience of walking the ditches of the Cohanzick River with my Dad. It breaks my heart to see that the places we used for so long are no longer accessible due to the greed of those who disregard our traditions. We are counting on the new generations to keep the stories alive and make a change.